SNOWED IN

The 5th

Murray Barber P.I.

Case

By

Julie Burns Sweeney

Copyright 2017

Published by Lulu.com

ISBN: 978-0-244-31165-0

CHAPTER ONE

Murray could feel his wheels starting to slip as they tried to grip the road. Snow was falling and the view ahead was fast turning to shades of white. Why had he thought it would be a good idea to cut across the moor? When he had heard about the accident on the main road he should just have done the sensible thing and stayed in Exeter.

The day had started off well enough, he had driven Jenny up to the airport to catch her flight to Tokyo. They had sat and eaten a tasty lasagna lunch while they waited to hear if her journey would be cancelled due to the incoming weather. After some delay, she had kissed him goodbye for the next three days and boarded, leaving Murray to make his journey home. That's when he made the mistake of turning off the main road and its growing traffic jam and heading up onto the moor. Then the snow began to fall.. and fall...

He had crossed the moor many times, usually in lovely sunny weather where the full beauty of the views could be appreciated, but now as his wheels continued to slip and spin, the panoramic view was the last thing on his mind. He decided to pull onto the side of the road, hoping that he wasn't about to slide into a snow covered ditch, and gather his bearings. He was pretty sure that there were crossroads ahead and a family-run inn just beyond. He turned off his engine, dragged himself out of the warmth of his car and climbed onto a stone outcrop that stood beside the road. Through the growing blizzard conditions he could just make out the lights and smoke funnels that rose from a roaring fireplace. The best thing he could do now was head towards the inn and hope for a room until the weather subsided. He considered using the blanket he kept in the boot to cover his engine but, apart from the fact he didn't want to hang around until it cooled down enough to place the blanket over it, he realized that if there was no room at the inn, he may well need that blanket himself in his car for the night.

So, with crisp snow crunching below his feet he marched down the lane in the direction of the smoking fireplace. He had passed the crossroads when another car came into sight. It, like his own, was parked up at the side of the road, the road which was fast disappearing into a white oblivion. Murray tapped on the window and smiled as the middle-aged woman inside nearly jumped out of her skin. She returned his gaze with a petrified stare from behind her large rimmed glasses. Murray motioned for her to wind down the window as he tried to ask her if she was alright? After some more encouragement, she finally wound the window down half an inch.

"Don't worry, I'm not a mass murderer on a wild rampage! I'm stuck too, just back there. I know there's an inn a bit further on, did you want to hike along to it with me? We might manage to squeeze a couple of rooms out of them till the weather breaks?"

She still looked hesitant but after staring at her

surroundings she gathered her handbag, pulled her coat tight around herself and clambered out of her car.

"I'm Murray. Think I should have stayed in town but a bit late now! Where were you heading?" He was asking in his friendliest voice but the lady didn't seem to be keen on divulging anything personal.

"I was heading west on the A30. Maybe I should have stayed on the main road too!" She finally managed a weak smile as she spoke with a northern accent. "You say there's an inn down the road?"

"Yeah, not too far if I remember rightly. You don't sound local?" He was sure it wasn't Liverpudlian or Yorkshire, maybe Manchurian? "You can't be on holiday at this time of year?"

"Just a short getaway. What about you?" The two of them were walking along the road, fighting with the blowing snow which was getting tossed around in the wind.

"Dropped my girlfriend off at the airport. Think she's the lucky one, heading half way around the globe, should be safe from this weather!"

"How long do you think this weather will last?" the lady asked.

"Who knows? We don't get this very often. Not more than a day or two I shouldn't think. Does that disrupt your plans?" Murray noticed that she was looking concerned. As the road rounded a rocky tor they could see the inn ahead of them.

"Ah ha! Lights are on, must be someone home." It was a welcome sight and the two of them picked up their pace. When they reached the big front door, Murray gave it a loud rap. In front of the building stood a box van and a snow covered hatchback. "Other stranded travelers?" he grimaced as he glanced around them. He caught sight of a woman peering out of the store door at the side of the main inn. He got just a quick glimpse of her straight black hair and dark skin and brightly coloured red sweater before she backed out of sight. "Well someone's home!"

"Yes, do you think we should go over there and ask her for help?..." But as Murray's companion spoke the front door was opened and the friendly face of a large middle-aged woman beamed at them.

"Oh dear! Come on in. Are you stuck on the road aswell? This weather's come in fast hasn't it?" She had deep west country tones which rang out warmly as she stepped back to allow them room to enter. They stomped the snow from their shoes and followed the landlady to the desk. "Right, I'm Cath. We're doing the rooms cheap, I take it you'll need one for the night?"

"Oh, we're not together. We just met on the lane. Do you have two singles?" Cath chuckled as she opened the register.

"Yes my dear! Sorry 'bout that. What's your name my love?"

"Hooper, Valerie Hooper. How much is it?"

"Twenty pounds my dear, just to cover costs. Can't leave you out in this weather now can we?" Valerie signed the book. "Now you sir?"

"Murray Barber." He was tempted to continue

with 'private investigator' like he did each time he answered his phone, but he managed to stop himself. With registration complete, Cath gave them a quick guided tour on the way to their rooms.

"There's the dining room, we'll be serving in about half an hour. And through there is the tv and round this corner you'll probably be glad to see the bar!" Cath chuckled again, a short deep chuckle, as she climbed the staircase. Murray knew where he intended to spend the evening, in front of that roaring fire in the bar with a pint in his hand! At the top of the staircase Cath gave the first key to Valerie.

"Here you are my dear. Room Two for you. And Mr Barber, here you go, Room Four." She handed him the second key. "I'll let you get settled and as I said, dinner starts in half an hour."

Cath left them there and Murray seeing that Valerie still looked quite pale, regardless of the freezing weather and warm as toast inn, decided to offer her a friendly hand.

"Dinner's on me if you'll join me?" he smiled.

"Oh? That's very nice of you. Erm, sure, why not?" She nodded and entered her room. With her door shut, Murray entered his own. It was light and bright with what would normally be a fantastic view across the moor but now just looked a dazzle of white moving dots. He had brought nothing but his mobile and wallet but there were clean towels in the ensuite so Murray decided on a quick freshen up and then to send a couple of 'I'm ok' messages.

A quick call to his parents proved that the weather

was far spread to the west and a text to Jeff informed him that at least he'd have to behave himself if he was stuck in the middle of nowhere for the night! Jeff himself would be working all night, there was an attempted rape case to deal with, 'not pleasant' were the words his C.I.D. friend used to describe it. Murray glanced at his watch, Jenny would still be in the air, no doubt she would contact him when she landed. That just left him to contemplate phoning Michelle. She was the old school friend which he had met up with at the reunion a couple of months back. Something that shouldn't have happened, happened and it had happened once more since. Infact, he reluctantly admitted he was hoping it was going to happen again during the next three days. He had intended on turning up at the Hayloft restaurant where she worked as manager but now it seemed his plans were being thrown into the snow as it were. Maybe it was for the best? He had moments of guilt, deep pangs of gut wrenching guilt, when he could see himself becoming one of the very people that his clients paid him to follow and snoop on, the 'unfaithful other halves'. Jenny deserved better than that. Jenny with her scatterbrain and ever-changing hair who still managed to work a highly skilled PA job. So why did he keep thinking of Michelle? Recently divorced, laid back Michelle with one colour hair who knew him so well, knew about his gift of hearing the dead... Yes, he could relax more with Michelle, she was fun in a whole different way to Jenny... No phonecall, not yet anyway, now it was time to eat...

CHAPTER TWO

Murray sat himself down at the table next to the window and glanced around the dining room at his fellow stranded travelers. There was a tall willowy man in a suit, it looked as though he'd just arrived as Cath was still explaining the layout to him. Another, a sturdy man with jet black hair and grubby jeans, was sat near the door tucking into his bread roll, one of which was placed on each person's table. Behind Murray sat a couple, he noticed that she had long legs and long dark brown hair. He looked older with stubble around his chin.

"What would you like sir?" A round-faced teenager had strolled up to Murray's table, a small notepad and pencil in her hands.

"Oh, er... I'm supposed to be dining with Miss Hooper. Can I hang on for a minute?"

"Sure, don't think any of us are going anywhere!" She smiled at him.

"It's a lovely place. Many staff here?"

"No. Just me and Mum and Dad, he's cooking. We have more in the summer of course but we're not usually this busy this time of year."

"Bit of a windfall with the snowfall eh?" Even Murray didn't think he'd sounded funny but he still got a smile from his waitress.

"Karenza, if Mr Barber doesn't want to order just

yet at least offer him a drink." Cath walked past and smiled at Murray as she disappeared into the kitchen.

"Would you like a drink Mr Barber?" Karenza repeated.

"Ah, my guest." Valerie had just descended the stairs and, spotting Murray, sat herself down at his table. "Shall we order?" he asked.

So, with food and beverages brought to their table by the friendly Karenza, the two of them realised just how hungry they had become and tucked into their farmhouse cottage pies.

"I don't see our Indian friend? Perhaps she works in the kitchen?" Valerie was glancing around at the other diners.

"No, Karenza said it's only her and her parent's

here. Odd?"

"Mmm, oh well. Let's hope we can get out of here tomorrow."

"You in a hurry to get somewhere? Short getaway I think you said?" Murray's phone beeped as he spoke. "Uh, sorry!" he pulled it out of his pocket and glanced at its screen. A message from Michelle. He'd check it after dinner.

"Oh, just visiting a friend. Is that your girlfriend arriving at her destination?"

"Erm, no. Work." Murray lied.

"Oh, what do you do?" Valerie sounded genuinely interested.

"I'm a private investigator. Not as exciting as it sounds believe me!" Valerie had stopped eating and was staring at him across the table. Without looking around, Murray felt that everyone else had cast a glance in his direction aswell.

"Really?" She finally asked.

"I'm not working now! It's mainly a lot of sitting in the car watching to be honest. Why, you want to hire me?" Murray sat back having finished his last mouthful. Valerie shook her head.

"No, I doubt I could afford you anyhow!" She then leant forward towards him. "Maybe you could solve the case of the disappearing Indian lady!"

"We DID see her didn't we?"

"Yes." She frowned and sipped her coffee. "Definitely we did!"

After dinner, Valerie declined Murray's offer of a drink in the bar and instead headed to her room to relax. The willowy man followed her upstairs and the sturdy man shook some car keys and pulling his hood up over his head, let himself out the front door. Murray watched him from the window, surely he wasn't going to try and move his vehicle? The snow was still falling. All the man did was walk around the van double checking that all the doors were locked. Murray wondered what precious cargo the man had? But he didn't wonder for long as he felt the bar calling....

As he strolled into the rustic style bar, the couple were already there awaiting the barman. It sounded to Murray like they had been arguing but they fell awkwardly silent as he turned the corner into their view. Did he's being a private investigator make them nervous? Surely there'd be only one reason for that? He smiled at them as he entered.

"Are we open yet?" he joked. "Doesn't look like any of us'll be driving tonight!"

The man smiled back, the woman turned and glared out of the window. Then rescue arrived in the form of Karenza. First waitress, now barmaid! Probably chambermaid in the morning!

"Right people, what can I get you?"

Murray stepped back to let the lady go first.

"Samantha?" Her partner asked.

"JD and coke." It was short and curt.

"We'll have two JD and coke's please." Karenza served them and they sat down by the window.

"And you Mr Barber?"

"Oh, I'll have a house red please. Erm.. did I see a lady out by the store on our way in?" Karenza poured his drink and then watched him.

"Lady?" she asked slowly.

"Yeah, could have sworn we saw an Indian lady, in a bright red jumper, out by the store?" Karenza shook her head.

"No, no lady like that. You must have been seeing things. There's just us here there is. Or at least, she never knocked to come in." Her mouth was smiling at him but Murray noted that her eyes were still watching him closely. He glanced around the bar to break the moment, Samantha and 'friend' were barely speaking and casting sideways glances in his direction. He began to wonder if there was something about him that looked menacing? Or did they just all have secrets they wanted to keep from him? Murray decided to ignore them and took a look at the old photo that hung behind the bar. It was a family portrait of three men and three women all dressed in period clothes. The women had long skirts and the men high collars and waistcoats. The couple in the centre looked a generation older, the parents maybe?

"So who are they then?" Murray asked as he sipped his wine. Karenza leant on the bar, seemingly relaxing, and stared at the picture.

"Previous owners of this place. There's quite a story comes with them there is." Karenza had the same strong west country tones as her mother. "Now, I'm not sure who's who in the photo, Dad does, but one of them two girls murdered the other one and now she haunts this place, whistling along the landings! Though I've never heard her."

"Really?" Murray couldn't help but be intrigued.

This sort of thing was right up his alley! "The murdered girl still walks, searching for revenge eh? When did this happen then? Looks pre-war to me?"

"Well the guilty girl, Emily, was hanged in November 1927. She murdered her sister in the January, in the snow like it is now! Celia I think her name was? Apparently she was coming back from Dart Farm, just across the ravine, and Emily pushed her into the stream, bashing her head on the rocks. Then she went running for help all upset like."

"Sounds horrific. Why did she do it?"

"Jealousy! Celia was married to him.." she pointed to the tall young man in the photo. "..and Emily was dead jealous because she wanted him." Murray stared again at the photo. He wasn't sure if he believed any of Karenza's story but at least it was entertaining. "So who are the other's? The parents I take it, and who?"

"Well, there's the two sisters, her and her. They're the parents, those two, yeah they look older don't they? He's James, the husband and that man is William I think? He was their brother. He worked at Dart Farm but it was James who was taking over the Inn from the parents. Strange they should hand it to the son-in-law and not their own blood?"

"Mmm? And Celia whistles as she wanders around in here does she?"

"Apparently! But like I say, I've never heard her." At this point the van man with his jet black hair returned and ordered a pint. He nodded politely at Murray.

"Evening."

"Evening." Murray said back. "Van's not damaged is it?"

"No, van's ok. Just checking that was all." The man didn't sound like he wanted to talk about his van so Murray thought better of asking any more. He glanced back over towards the couple by the window. They were talking quietly but she still didn't look happy. Seeing the two of them together however, did remind him of his phone message. He put his glass back on the bar and pulled out his phone. It read..

'Can't get to the restaurant it's snowing! Did Jenny catch her flight? Thought I might put my boots on and go for a walk, might get lost though.. end up at your place...????' He smiled to himself. Typical! He sent a text back.. 'Sorry, stuck on moor! Jenny gone.

Will let u know if I get back. x'. He then took his glass and sat himself down on the settee and stared once more at the old photo hanging behind the bar. No, he couldn't hear any whistling...

"Well I must say, it's all very quiet in here!" Cath came bounding into the bar with another round-faced man who shared a great resemblance to Karenza. "Has everybody got a drink in their hand?" She glanced round as everyone raised their glasses. "Oh good! Shame about the weather but we'll just have to make the best of it won't we?" She poured herself and her husband a drink and wandered over to the van man. "You ok Mr Finlay?" As his wife sat herself down and started a conversation, a little one-sided, with Mr Finlay, her husband stood watching Murray. It took him a moment to become aware of the eyes fixed upon himself but once he did, he got to his feet and stepped back over to the bar.

"Your daughter's been telling me the story behind that photo." Murray pointed to the wall behind Karenza.

"Oh, that old story." The man seemed to relax but Murray was beginning to feel extremely self conscious. "Sad really but I can't say I believe in all that ghost stuff."

"We've had a few guests though that say they've heard whistling upstairs. Remember that woman Jim, the one that said she was kept up all night by it?"

"Yeah, and she ended up with a discount! A big fiddle if you ask me Love."

At this point the couple by the window got to their feet and returned their glasses to the bar and upon saying 'goodnight' headed off upstairs to their room. Jim turned back to Murray.

"So you're a private eye are you?" he asked with his head cocked back.

"It pays the bills!"

"You following those two are you?" he nodded up the stairs.

"No! Should I be?" Murray joked.

"Jim don't you go saying things like that!"

"Well." Jim refilled his ale glass. "They come here quite regularly those two but, well, it's obvious ain't it?"

"I did wonder." Murray let out a laugh. "They didn't seem at all keen on my announcing my business! I expect they're sweating a bit being stuck out here like this? Someone at home getting suspicious maybe?"

"Is that the sort of work you do then?" Jim was now leaning on the bar. Mr Finlay was sat silently, listening intently.

"For the most part. None of it's that exciting, not like the tv programmes!"

"You on a case now then?" Somehow Murray felt he was being interrogated. He first thought to be honest, he did have jobs on the go but they were sat in his notebook which itself was sat on his computer desk at home. But if these people were wondering what he was up to, if they thought he was 'onto' them, then maybe he'd have some fun?

"I've got a couple of jobs I'm working on at the

moment." He glanced from one of them to the other. After a pause Mr Finlay got his feet, he took his keys from his pocket once more, along with a packet of cigarettes, and headed one last time out to his van.

"What about him?" Karenza asked. "Is he up to anything?"

"I doubt it! But he's very concerned about whatever's in the back of that van of his!" Murray once again laughed and was joined by Karenza.

"What about the other guests?"

"Karenza!" Cath sounded quite horrified.

"I don't think anyone's guilty of anything terrible. Nothing to keep you awake at night anyhow!"

"Well apart from your lady friend, we've only got that rep guy here. You can't get anymore mundane that a sales rep!" Karenza was enjoying herself regardless of her parent's disapproving glances. Murray decided it was time to quit while he was ahead, so he finished his glass and headed upstairs.

CHAPTER THREE

Murray lay on the bed. He wasn't ready to get undressed or sleep yet, it was only eleven after all. He took out his phone and dialled his mum again. She had fallen on the ice before and hopefully was taking more care this time.

With that call out of the way, Murray decided to give Jeff, his friend from C.I.D. a call.

"... How on earth did you manage to get stuck up there Murray? What made you take the high road?"

"I was just trying to avoid an accident and get home! Anyway, it's not a bad place, nice wine but strange people!"

"What do you mean?"

"Ah, I don't know really. Just a bit odd! Could've sworn we saw an Indian girl on the way in but everyone's denying she exists! And some bloke who acts like he's carrying the crown jewels in the back of his van!"

"As long as the place ain't haunted! Here, why don't you send Donny and Marie out to have a snoop around? They'd soon tell you what was going on!"

"Ha ha! I don't think ghosts have a homing devise built in! They'll never find me stuck out here. And it's Ali and Rita! They get really fed up with you taking the mickey you know!"

"Do they? I'll have to watch myself then, don't want to gain a poltergeist or two!"

"Well look, I only called to let you know where I am. Have a good night."

"Yeah, you too!"

Murray had ended the call just as his phone was beeping to tell him a message had arrived, it was from Jenny. She'd arrived in Tokyo safely and the weather was cool but not a hint of snow anywhere! She was looking forward to a spot of shopping in between meetings and had he managed to get home before the snow hit? He returned the text letting her know he hadn't but hopefully, if the snow stopped falling before morning, he'd make it back tomorrow. He was then interrupted by a rap at the door. Murray put his head against the door and whispered.

"Who's there?"

"Me, Valerie." Murray opened the door to see a pale looking Valerie stood on the landing. "Sorry, can I talk to you?"

"Sure, come in." He stepped back and with her arms folded, she came inside. "You ok?"

"Not really." She turned and forced a smile at him. "Can I trust you?"

"Yeah, course. What's wrong?"

"I'm not sure where to start? I... er, I'm running

away. I saw something I wish I hadn't and now.. well, I think they're after me."

"Who are? Sorry, sit down and start from the beginning." Murray sat down on the edge of the bed beside her.

"Oh..." Valerie wasn't crying but she looked terrified. "I live in Manchester, on a big estate. We all overlook each other you know, and I was just going about my business, doing my dishes.. and I glanced across opposite and ..in the flat down over from me... I saw someone get killed. Knifed. In their flat." She was staring at Murray wide eyed. "But they saw me."

"Did you see them see you?"

"Yes. They looked straight at me. There were three of them but I can't really say what they looked like.

It happened so quickly but at the same time so slowly... I just dropped my cloth and I started crying and then I just grabbed my handbag and my keys and I fled. I knew it wouldn't take them long to get round to my flat. I just started driving and I didn't even know where I was going to go... Then I thought of my sister, she lives in Newquay. I thought they're never gonna find me there. She doesn't even have the same name, she's been married. So I was heading down there when the snow started."

"You were heading west on the A30?" Suddenly her original look of fear when he had tapped on her car window made sense. And he'd said he wasn't a mass murderer! "You should be safe enough now. I take it you don't want to go home?"

"I can't. They'll wait for me. I know they will. I'll have to start again near my sister. I just wanted to talk to someone and you seemed safe enough."

"Thanks. Look, I've got a friend in C.I.D. You could talk to him. They could get your information back to the Manchester police and get it dealt with, you don't want to hide for the rest of your life?"

"Oh, I don't know about that? I'd have to think about it. I'm not sure I want to get involved officially. Can I... can I leave a statement with you, just incase something happens to me?"

"What do you mean?" Murray wasn't sure if he was getting the full story.

"I don't really know. Maybe I could leave a written note with you... it's just that... well, I thought I might have been followed? That's why I turned off the main road. It was probably just my mind, I've been so scared..."

"It's alright. No-one's going to get you here! Look, why don't you let me record you saying what happened on my phone? Then, when you get safely to your sister's, you can call me and tell me what you want to do next, ok?" He tried to look his most reassuring as she studied his face considering what to do.

"Ok." she finally said. So, with Murray holding his phone, she repeated her story, filling in as many details as she could recall. Once done, Murray played it back to her, checking it was ok. Appearing much more relaxed, Valerie apologized for disturbing him and putting all her problems into his lap. He told her not to worry and try and get some sleep. He'd have breakfast with her and then they'd walk back out to their cars and, weather permitting, he'd follow her as far as she wanted to Newquay. Valerie left to return to her room.

Murray took a deep breath and wandered over to the window. He stood there for a while. Should he call Michelle? It was dark outside even though everything was white. He thought 'what the hell' and dialled her number. As the line connected and rang he strained to see around the side of the building, there was a beam of light streaming dimly across the courtyard. It looked like the dipped headlights of a vehicle but surely no-one was mad enough to try and drive in this?

"Hello you!" Michelle's warm voice answered her phone.

"Hello you!" He answered still staring out of the window. "Sorry I never made it home tonight, tried a diversion away from an accident and got stuck! Nice inn though."

"You're not hurt?"

"No, no I'm safe and sound. Had a nice meal, nice glass or two of wine and now I'm just thinking of turning in for the night."

"Ah, all on your own?"

"Mmm, pity, it's a bit of a waste of a nice big comfy bed!"

"What are you doing now?"

"Erm, I'm watching out of my window.sorry, I know that's not what you're wanting to hear but, well..." Murray was straining now to see outside. "There are two men, I think they're men, outside with a four-wheel drive, jeepy thing. One of them's getting in... hang on, I think there's someone else already in the jeep? Where the hell are they going at this time of night in this weather?"

"Sounds a bit strange?"

"There are some strange thing's going on here I think!"

"Have you got Ali or Rita with you? Can't you send them out to find out what's going on?"

"No, wish they were here. He's driving off. Where the hell is he going at this time of night?"

"Can't you see who it is?"

"No... It's too dark, just see shadows really. And big coats!... oh well, they've gone down the lane whoever they were. Maybe I'll have a nose out there in the morning? They've gone the same way as back to my car. The other guy's come back in.. he must be the landlord?"

"So what are you going to do now then?" There was a touch of teasing in her voice.

"Ooh, maybe I'll strip down and have a quick shower and then tuck myself up in bed. What about you?"

"Maybe I'm already naked?..."

"Hang on... "

"What? What are you doing?"

"Not that! There's someone out on the landing. Maybe it's the same guy from outside?"

"Murray, you're hopeless!"

"If you were here, or I was there, believe me it'd be different. They could move mountains outside and I wouldn't be interested! But I'm here... hang on, I'm gonna try opening the door a crack..." Murray peered out on to the landing. A few doors along he heard the sound of a door close quietly. He couldn't see whose room it was, not the landlord's though. He stepped out, his phone held to his chest, and peered over the bannister. No-one in sight. It wasn't silent though, he could hear the gentle melody of someone whistling. Was it coming from downstairs or one of the rooms? He wasn't sure. He stepped back into his room and closed his door carefully.

"Someone's come in but I didn't see who it was. Someone's whistling!"

"Whistling?" Michelle repeated.

"Mmm? Wonder if it's the ghost?"

"What ghost? You said Rita and Ali weren't with you?"

"No, there's a photo down in the bar and apparently one of the girls in it haunts this place, people occasionally hear her whistling."

"Well then you should be able to hear her! Do you think it's the ghost?"

Murray had stopped still, he was staring across his room towards the en-suite.

"I think she may be in my room?"

"Oh Murray! Don't you cheat on me with a ghost now!" Michelle was laughing down the phone.

"Ha ha! Love I'm gonna go ok. I'll get back to you in the morning, hopefully be on the road home?"

"Ok, you take care. Hopefully we can get together tomorrow night, if I have to go to the restaurant I'll try and get away early. Bye hun."

With the call ended, Murray stepped over towards

the bathroom. Then he spun around, the whistling started again behind him, near the door.

"Hello?" he spoke quietly but without any fear in his voice.

"Another one that can hear me. Been a while."

"Celia?" There was no immediate answer. "Celia? Is that you?"

"Why do people always think I'm Celia?"

"You're not Celia? Then .. you're Emily?"

"Can you hear me talking? Usually it's just my whistling?"

"I can hear you loud and clear. Are you Emily?"

"I might be."

"Then you didn't murder your sister." Again there was silence. "Hello? Have you gone?" Murray glanced around his room, not that he expected to see anything, his gift only allowed him to hear the dead.

"You can't see me then?" She hadn't moved away from the door.

"No. Just hear you."

"I didn't kill my sister. But how do you know that?"

"Because you're here talking to me now! I'm no expert but I have learn't that murderer's tend to go straight to hell, do not pass go and do not collect two hundred pounds and don't contact the living!"

"Oh!" She sounded a little taken aback. "So I can't scare you either then?"

"No, 'fraid not! Do you want to tell me what did happen to your sister?" Murray sat himself back down on his bed, it was turning into a very long night.

"I would love to tell you what happened to my sister! But I'm afraid I don't know that myself."

"You don't know? Surely you've found out since you died? It's been ... what? Over eighty years?"

"I don't know what happened."

"Haven't you spoken to your sister? She'd know exactly what happened to her, who killed her?"

"Would she? I haven't made contact with any of them. No-one believed me, they all thought I was guilty. They all watched me hang."

"Your sister will know it wasn't you. They probably all know now, are they all dead now? And also, the real murderer would have known you were innocent." Yet again the room fell silent. Was Emily considering what Murray was saying? "Why don't you go where ever it is you lot go and see if you can find them? Then you can find out the whole truth."

"No, I don't want to." She sounded defiant, her voice gliding across the room towards the window. If only Murray could get hold of Rita and Ali, they wouldn't fuss about going and sorting this out. "They've never come to me."

"Ok. Don't then. Stay and suffer if that's what makes you happy." Murray sat back on the bed and rested his head on the headboard. "Be forever guilty!"

"You're mean! Why don't you help me work out who really did it? I heard you helping that lady just now."

"You listen in? Does that mean you know what else is going on in this place?"

"Lots goes on in this place!"

"Maybe..." Murray sat forward again. "Maybe I'll try and help you if you can tell me if there is an Indian lady here?"

"Oh, her! Yes, I think they call her Shani? Something like that."

"She IS here? Why are they all lying about her then? Shani you say? Who is she?"

"Don't know, she hasn't been here long. Now can you help me?"

"Uh.. Look, you do realize that there's no evidence left on this side, life? The truth will be on your side... Where is this Shani?"

"Downstairs in the private quarters last time I saw her... I told you, I don't want to see anyone..."

"Ok. Why don't you sit down and tell me your version of what happened on that day in January

1927...."

CHAPTER FOUR

"It had been a hard winter. The snow had laid on the ground for about ten days. Most of the local workers came to the inn at the end of a days hard graft. The roaring fireplace kept them warm and the cider quenched their thirst. Mother and Father were getting the cottage ready to move into the coming spring. They were letting James and my sister, Celia, take over the reins of the inn, though I'd still be living and working there. William, my brother, was living at the farm where he was working. He and my father were always falling out. Father always said William needed to be more responsible, he'd never let him run the family business until he'd sorted himself out. Don't get me wrong, he wasn't a bad young man, but he drank too much and spent his earnings too freely. Had a bit of a temper too but no more than most young men. Father was sure he would come good one day, then he'd hand him back the inn. Not sure how James really felt about that? Think he was determined to show Father he was the better landlord...."

"Sounds like some family rivallry going on?" Murray was still sat comfortably on his bed. Emily's voice was coming from the bottom corner.

"Undercurrents maybe. It had been a bright

morning and Celia had set off to the farm to collect a few supplies. Just what she could carry. Milk and eggs. James had gone to collect a side of pig from Hurler's yard. Then it had started to snow again. James wasn't back and I was getting worried that Celia would be stranded down the farm. I decided to go look for her, I thought if I met her half way we could help each other back..."

"How long did it take you to find her?"

"Not that long. We always went down the ravine and across the river, there are some solid stones that enable you to get across quite easily. Then up the other side and along the lane to the farm. I could see her lying there from the top of the hill. The falling snow had started to cover her in a soft white blanket...." Emily had slowed, lost in the memory. "She looked quite peaceful really."

"So she had been there a while when you found her?"

"Why do you say that?"

"Because of the snow settling on top of her. Were there any other footprints?"

"No.... not that I remember? I suppose they would have been covered up by the falling snow anyhow?"

"Quite possibly? And you didn't see anybody? You didn't pass anyone?" Emily was silent for a few moments.

"No. I don't remember seeing anyone. I think that's what they said during my trial? Only my footprints."

"Not a lot to go on is it? Do you remember anyone hating...that's a strong word, but did anyone have a reason to harm your sister?"

"She was beautiful my sister. She was sweet and caring. James was a lucky man."

"And you apparently were jealous?"

"No I wasn't. Not at all. We were very close, I could never have harmed her."

"Tell you what, it's too late now..." Murray glanced at the bedside clock to see the digital display showing it was three fifteen. "...but tomorrow I'll give Jeff a call and see if he can dig up any old case notes. He's a policeman. I don't have my laptop with me so I can't do any research myself. You do realize though, that this would all be so easy if you'd just go and talk to your sister?"

"What's a 'laptop'?" Murray laughed gently as he sat forward.

"Now even my ghostly friends know what a computer is! You really have kept yourself shut away haven't you?"

"This is my home. I want to stay here."

"Well I'm not asking you to leave but I am going to try and get some sleep. I may have to make a treacherous drive home tomorrow."

He wasn't sure what time it was when he was suddenly woken from his intermittent slumber. Shani and knifings were swimming around in his mind. He sat up sharply as he heard the sudden crack of wood. He slid out of bed, grabbing his jeans, and glanced out of the window. There at the store door was the flickering glow of flames. Jim, Cath and Karenza were already down in the courtyard with buckets and shovels, their west country tones rising up through the freezing night air. Murray blinked and wiped the steam which was forming on the inside of his window pane. Acting quickly, he pulled on his trousers, jumper and any other item of clothing he could find and headed out along the landing and down the stairs to the front door. Outside the snow was still falling but Murray ignored the weather and ran around to the side of the inn to see what he could do to help...

For nearly twenty-five minutes they threw buckets of snow and water at the flames. There was little chance of a fire engine reaching them on these roads with the snow still falling. Both Mr Finlay the van man and the willowy sales rep had joined them to beat the fire and they had managed finally to put it out. Murray stood back and took a deep cold breath. Karenza and the sales rep headed back inside and Mr Finlay, not surprisingly, went to check his van first before following them. The logs had stood at the front of the store and now most of them were sodden. It'd be a while before they were any good to burn. It crossed Murray's mind that they wouldn't have burst into flames on their own. Was someone out here in the early morning cold having a sneaky cigarette? Or did someone start the fire on purpose? His eye had caught sight of a partially burnt item lying on the floor amongst the ashes.

"Thankyou so much for your help. We don't usually require our guests to put their lives at risk when they stay here!" Jim was sounding relieved that it was over but as Murray turned towards him to answer, he noticed that keen watchfulness in the man's eye.

"Thank God no-one's been hurt eh?" Murray reached down and picked up the partially burnt bright red jumper.

"No! Just half a tonne of logs ruined!" Cath was just as watchful. "Come on, let's get inside out of this snow in the warm and get the kettle on. I think we could all do with warming up. Here, leave that rubbish here Mr Barber, we'll sort it out later when the sunlight rises."

Murray dropped the jumper but said nothing. Had Shani been in the fire? Was she hurt? Had she started the fire? Were they keeping her here against her will? Maybe she was an illegal immigrant or some sort of people trafficking thing? His mind was spinning the theories were coming so fast. The exhilaration of fighting the fire and the lack of any decent sleep were sending his thought's off on wild paths. He needed to get inside and drink that hot drink that Cath was offering and let his mind sort itself into some order....

CHAPTER FIVE

Murray didn't go back to bed. It was a quarter to six by the time they returned indoors after putting out the fire. He sat in the tv room staring blankly at the news channel as it hummed away quietly in the corner of the room. He hugged his hot coffee and tried to think of nothing in order to let his mind clear itself. He wasn't at all sure what was going on at this inn but he was sure he was going to find out. He waited for the clock to tick past six before he climbed the stairs back to his room for some privacy to phone Jeff.

"You still stuck out in the snow Murray?" Jeff was half laughing and half asleep. "I'm still tucked up in my bed!"

"Sorry mate, is it your day off?" Murray was at the window staring at the scene from the night's events.

"It's alright, Kate's getting me breakfast in bed! What do you want?"

"Someone to talk common sense to me! You're never gonna believe the night I've had?"

"You wanna tell me about it while I wait for my bacon and eggs?"

"It's where to start? Valerie Hooper, the woman I met in the lane on my way here yesterday, she says she saw a man murdered opposite her flat in Manchester yesterday and now she's running from the men who committed it. She's made a recording on my phone about what she saw, she's worried something's gonna happen to her..."

"She needs to get to a station, report it straight away then it's too late for them to stop her. Does she know who they are?"

"Not by name but she gave a reasonable description of one of them. She's got it in her head they're already following her. I'll have a word with her at breakfast. Then of course there's this ghost, there's an old photo in the bar ..."

"You and your voices! No sign of Ali and Rita yet then?" Jeff said the names clearly.

"No. But can I ask a favour? You couldn't see if there's any archive stuff on the murder of Celia Gidleigh? Her sister Emily Tremwall was hanged for the offence in 1927. Thing is, she wasn't guilty. If she'd only go and talk to her sister I wouldn't need to bother you but she won't. I'd like to know if there's anything useful still worth reading, I haven't got my laptop with me."

"Hang on, I'm still writing that down... I can have a look but that's an old case. Maybe something on-line, you use the archive sites don't you?"

"Yeah, you know the usual ones. You sure you don't mind?"

"No, can't promise anything though. Has the rest of your night been quiet?"

"Oh, apart from the fire, sure!"

"Fire?"

"This Indian girl I saw yesterday when I arrived, well, Emily says she is here and her name is Shani. But I don't understand why everyone's denying she exists? And last night there was a fire in the store outside, where I had seen her, and after we put it out....."

"No fire service?....oh, I suppose they'd never get up there?"

"Not easily! Anyhow, in the ashes I found the very top, a bright red one, that I'd seen her wearing."

"You think she's been hurt? They're not hiding a body are they?"

"I don't know. I can't get my head round any of it at the moment. I'm dead tired and that's not supposed to be funny!"

"Tell you what, I'll check this old case out for you, I'll get in touch with Manchester and I'll run a few checks on that inn and it's owners. Keep your phone on, I'll get back to you as soon as, ok?"

"Ah, thanks Jeff, you're a mate and a half."

It was time for breakfast so Murray washed his face and headed downstairs to the dining room. The couple, Samantha and 'friend', were already seated by the window. They cast him a quick glance as he entered the room. 'Where were they when the fire was raging?' Murray wondered. 'Making up their lover's tiff maybe?' The willowy sales rep was sat in the corner and, just as Murray sat himself down, Mr Finlay came in through the front door. 'No doubt checking that bloody van again!' thought Murray. 'Maybe I'll get a look at that van myself when I go out?' As Karenza carried round the coffee Murray noticed that only Valerie hadn't descended for breakfast. Maybe he should go and wake her? It had stopped snowing and he wanted to get out and check the road as soon as possible. He declined the coffee and went up to her room.

He first knocked gently but with no reply knocked again somewhat harder. Still no reply. He stared at the door handle wondering whether to go ahead and walk in her room?

"Hello." Emily's voice sprung from beside him on the landing. Murray jumped and then turned towards where he gathered she was standing.

"Oh, hello. I've...er, had a word with my policeman friend." He kept his voice to a whisper. "He's going to look into the archives of your case today for us."

"Oh that's very good of him. Do you think he'll find anything? Something that was overlooked at the time?"

"Who knows? Can you do me a favour as you're here?"

"What?"

"Have a look in this room and see if Miss Hooper is ok. She hasn't come down for breakfast and I can't get an answer."

"Oh, ok. Hang on..." Murray stood back and leant against the bannister. "There's nobody in there. Maybe she got up early?"

"Bugger!" Murray stared up the landing. "Did you see her leave?"

"No, can't say I did."

"What about our Indian lady, Shani? Is she alright or was she in that fire last night?"

"Shani? Oh, I'll have to go and check. I haven't seen her this morning."

"What have you been doing?.. No, maybe I just shouldn't ask questions like that?" Murray started to head back downstairs. "I'm going to grab a quick breakfast and then I'm going to walk back out to the cars, mine and Valerie's. Can you let me know if you find either of them?"

"Ok, I'll go look."

Having eaten breakfast, a full English, Murray

pulled on his jacket and started out up the lane in the direction of the abandoned cars. He glanced at Mr Finlay's van but that could wait till he returned. He soon noticed that he was unwittingly walking along the tyre tracks left by the four-wheeled jeep that had mysteriously visited the inn during the early hours. He stopped and looked along the tracks. There were infact four tracks, was that front and back wheels or one set in each direction? Murray was no expert but he decided he would see where they went. He started walking again, he noted that Valerie's car was still where they had left it and still covered in undisturbed snow. She hadn't returned here. He continued on along the tracks and soon reached the crossroads. He stood and stared. The tracks turned off to the right. He looked to the right but all he could see was snow covered moorland. He looked for the nearest rock to climb on, carefully so not to slip off and break a limb, he climbed up and searched the horizon to see where the jeep could have been heading. Could he see wafts of smoke? Not the big black kind that emanated from full on blazes, but small puffs like those from a chimney? Was there a house down there? He jumped back down and continued to his own car. He wasn't sure whether it was worth trying to reach the house or not. It depended if he was going to be stuck on this moor for another day.

  He found his own car also covered in a coating of fresh snow. It's wheels were four inches deep in the stuff. He pulled open his door and hunted for his spare phone charger, he certainly didn't want to lose contact with the outside world! He then decided to turn over the engine so sat in his driving seat and bounced his foot gently on the accelerator. Murray sat with his eyes shut, he could easily drift off to sleep except his peace was disturbed by the ringing of his mobile. It was a call from Jenny.

"Hi Babe! I haven't woken you up have I? I'm thinking it's mid-morning there or have I got my time zones all wrong? Oh, are you driving?.."

"Hi.. er no, erm, no I'm not driving I'm just turning my engine over. I'm still stuck in the snow...."

"Oh Babe, are you ok?.."

"Yeah, yeah I'm fine. How's Tokyo?"

"Fantastic! The meeting's going well, we've just broken for some lunch so I thought I'd sneak out and give you a quick call. They're all sooo polite out here! We're expecting to finish dead on four this afternoon. Gareth says they always finish spot on time which means plenty of time for shopping! He's going to show me the best places to shop! I thought I'd try and get you a nice silk shirt.. or maybe a kimono thingy? What do you think?...oh ok, be right there. Murray hun I've got to go. Speak to you again later. Love you."

"Love you...too." She had hung up. Murray threw his head back against his head rest and breathed out deeply. "What next?"

"I think you're supposed to put a hose in through the window if you want to do yourself in Murray my man! But we wouldn't recommend it!" Murray sat forward, a smile spreading across his face.

"Ali?" He stared out through his window and turned off his engine.

"Yeah man. You have no idea how hard it was to find you."

"How did you manage to find me? Or don't I want to know?"

"We dropped in on Jeff to see if he could give us any clues. He's got a nice place." Ali's voice came closer to the car window. "They were discussing decorating their spare bedroom as a nursery!"

"Ali! we agreed we weren't going to mention anything!"

"You agreed! I didn't say a word!"

"Hello Rita! Glad to hear your voice too!"

"Hi Murray. Best not say anything to Jeff till he tells you, eh? And how on earth did you get stuck up here on the moor?"

"I took a detour to avoid an accident ok! It's not my fault it snowed! I'm glad you two are here, you're not gonna believe what's going on."

"Come on then, tell us mate."

"Walk back with me to the inn and I'll explain..."

The three of them walked back to the crossroads, leaving only one set of footprints, where Murray told them about the visiting jeep and showed them the tyre tracks. Then there was the fire. He went on to explain that, as of this morning, there were two missing women. Shani and Valerie. And as they continued down towards the inn, Murray told them the story of Emily and the murder of her sister Celia.

As he entered the front door of the inn, Murray

was stopped by Cath.

"Oh, it's you. Any sign of your friend, Miss Hooper?" she asked.

"She hasn't been to her car. Has she not shown up back here yet?"

"No, not a sign of her. I wonder what we should do? Do you think I should phone the police? Maybe a bit longer eh? They usually say twelve hours.. or is it twenty four?"

"Maybe we should leave it until this afternoon. Then if there still hasn't been any sign I think we should definitely report it."

"What does she mean 'usually'? eh Murray man."

"Oh, ok. How are the roads anyhow?"

"Still pretty thick. I'll have another look this afternoon. Let's hope it doesn't snow again."

"Mmm. I have called Ben over at Dart Farm, see if he'll get his tractor out and do some clearing. He said he'd go out drekly if it don't start snowing, so let's hope shall we?"

"Yes, let's hope!" Murray went to go upstairs so he could continue his conversation with Ali and Rita without looking nuts but Cath called out once more after him.

"There'll be a light lunch menu if you start to get hungry. From twelve till two."

"Ah, thankyou!" Murray called back.

Once back in the safety of his room, Murray threw himself down on his bed and turned to speak to Ali and Rita.

"Right you two. Somewhere in this inn is Emily. Please don't scare the liv..erm, just don't scare her!

You know what I mean."

"You want us to go look for her? Or shall we go and search for her sister?" Rita was at the foot of the bed.

"No. That can wait. Her situation's not going to change. I'd rather the two of you searched this place from top to bottom for the two missing women. Shani, what I saw of her, is a petite, young pretty Indian girl and Valerie a middle-aged lady with long hair and large rimmed glasses, if she is still wearing them. For all I know, both these women's lives could be at risk. Hopefully I'm wrong. Do you mind?"

"Nah man. No worries, we'll go and search every nook and cranny. You gonna stay here?" Ali was still by the door.

"Yeah, I'm hoping Jeff's going to call me. And no, I promise I won't say a word! You're probably winding me up about Kate anyhow?"

"Never Murray mate! Right, don't go away.. oh yeah, sorry, you can't, you're stuck here aren't you! ha!"

"Go!"

With his two friends leaving his room in silence, Murray plugged his phone into it's charger and wondered if he should risk heading out to have a snoop around Finlay's van? He decided on calling Jeff first.

"Murray! How's the weather?"

"Er.. oh bugger! It's snowing."

"Don't worry, they're saying this should be the last of it, it's supposed to be turning to rain tonight. I'm just about to log onto the archives for your old murder case. I can tell you this much, your inn keeper's are clean, squeaky clean! Unless of course, they've just never been caught! Not even a parking ticket Murray. Sorry. As for Manchester, there's not been a stabbing reported. Has this Hooper woman turned up? I'd like to get some more details from her."

"No, no she hasn't. Quite concerned really. I have got her recording on my phone."

"Ah.... Could you send that to me? Via e-mail?"

"Sure."

"Great, then I can send it on to Manchester."

"Guess who's turned up?"

"Err..." Jeff thought for a moment. "Not Ali and Rita?"

"Yep!"

"How'd they find you?"

"Visited you! I've asked them to search this place from top to bottom for these two women. Had asked this Emily to do it but she hasn't come back to me yet. Think she live's in her own world a bit..."

"Er, Murray, if she's been dead for nearly a century I don't think she 'live's' in our world......"

With the call to Jeff over, Murray headed back out into the snow...

CHAPTER SIX

Outside Murray wandered over towards Finlay's

van. Finlay himself had just passed Murray on his way inside. The sales rep was starting to feel the frustration of being cooped up at the inn aswell, giving Jim some grief about the roads and complaining about the appointments he was missing. Murray looked at the van. It's windows were blacked out so he couldn't see inside, there could be anything in there? He noted the registration number. Glancing across at the hatchback parked next to it, he noted that number too. It probably belonged to the couple, Samantha and 'friend' but it was worth checking out. He strolled around the side of the inn with a feeling he was being watched. He let his eyes sweep the building but couldn't catch sight of anyone at the windows. He decided to carry on with his search.

There was a large truck parked in the courtyard by the store. Probably the owner's? He now had three numbers written on the palm of his hand. He stood and stared at the store where the fire had been. He was a little surprised to see how such a small amount of damage had been caused, superficial more than anything. They had been lucky.

A thought crossed his mind as he turned to return indoors, maybe Valerie had set the fire to create a distraction so that she could leave unseen? No, if that had been the case surely she would have driven her car away? He was back to square one, she was missing...

Once again back in the warmth of his room, Murray redialled Jeff's number.

"Sorry, me again! Can you run a couple of plates

for us?"

"Now? Hang on I'll have to sign in.... ok off you go, first number.." Murray gave the number of the truck first and Jeff confirmed it was registered to Jim at the inn's address. The hatch was next, and that was registered to a Colin Williams from Bude. Probably was the man from the couple. Murray then gave the registration of Finlay's van.

"...Bryan Finlay, Bryan with a 'y'. Mmm, what have we here... Done by customs for excess on his duty-free's. Handling stolen goods, handling fake goods. He's a bit of a character, think I might pass his details onto the other department? You say he's still there at the inn?"

"Yeah, and still checking his van regularly, must have something inside."

"You don't think he might have stepped up to human trafficking do you Murray?"

"In cahoots with the squeaky clean owners? Couple of body's to get rid of? Think I might try for another look at that van?"

"Is that all the vehicles? Except yours of course..."

"Yeah, mine and Valerie's are up the lane...hang on, where's the rep's car? Rep's have to have cars. He's starting to moan about being stuck here and missing appointments, so he must have a car. I need to go for another walk I think. Better wait till my phone's charged up though. Anything on Emily?"

"Very little. Newspaper article. Jealous woman hits her sister's head on the rocks then holds her unconscious head under the water in the stream till she drowns. Post mortem says that's how she died. Jury says it was the sister, Emily. Local's shocked, family grieving. Nothing much."

"Oh well. Thanks anyhow. I'm gonna grab some lunch and then go for a walk I think."

"Ok, keep in touch Murray."

Murray decided to sit down and have some lunch, he felt it would look a little too suspicious if he went straight back out to the vehicles sat outside. Besides, he quite fancied a steak and stilton pasty. Karenza brought it over with a smile on her face, but those eyes were still watchful. He was sat by the window with the snow gently falling outside, the other guests were nowhere to be seen.

"Murray!" Rita sat herself down next to him. "We

can't find either of your two ladies."

"Not on your side or ours Man!" Ali was sitting himself down opposite Murray, who couldn't answer them with Karenza stood in the kitchen doorway.

"There doesn't seem to be anything out of the ordinary here..."

"Except what's going on upstairs with that couple!" Ali was laughing out loud, not that anyone but Rita and Murray could hear him. "There is one heck of a row going on up there! His missus has gone over to see her husband and now they're screaming down the phone at each other. Caught out while stuck away from home! Some people do like to weave themselves a tangled web!" Murray was glad at this point that he couldn't say anything for he was acutely aware that he himself was weaving the beginings of one of those very webs...

With Karenza still stood within earshot, Murray finished his lunch and offered his plate back to the kitchen. Then, hopefully with Ali and Rita upon his heels, he headed upstairs to his room to gather his phone and jacket. Once behind the closed bedroom door, Murray turned to his friends.

"You still with me?"

"Oh, talking to us now!"

"Sorry Ali, you know what it's like..."

"Don't tease Ali. Ok Murray, there's no sign of those two women, not that we can find. So what now?"

"Was there anything left in Valerie's room, number two along the landing?"

"Didn't notice anything, nothing out of place. Do you want us to take another look?"

"If you don't mind Rita? Look for anything that shouldn't be there. If she got up and left on her own she would have taken all her stuff with her surely?"

"Ok man, we'll be back in a second.." Their voices trailed off and Murray unplugged his phone and pulled on his jacket.

"Are they friends of yours?" Emily's voice was barely more than a whisper coming from the far side of the bed.

"Emily?" Murray stopped. "Is that you? Where have you been?"

"About. I'm not used to seeing other.. ghosts."

"Don't worry about those two, they're harmless! And yes, they are friends of mine! You didn't find

Shani or Valerie then?"

"No, like your friend's said, they're not here. What are you doing about me? You said you believed I didn't kill Celia..."

"I DO believe you! And I haven't forgotten about you. It's just that these two women could be in danger, not meaning to offend but, well, it's too late to save you."

"You're not being very nice."

"I'm sorry. I don't mean to sound off..."

"Murray.... oh?"

"Rita? That was quick."

"Yes. Erm, her handbag is still in her room. Surely she would have taken that with her?"

"Too right she would have done. So, she's definitely in trouble. Oh... er, you haven't met Emily yet have you?"

"Hello Emily, I'm Rita and this is Ali. Murray's not very good at introductions but we've got used to that!"

"Oi! Can you just get the niceties over so we can get on?" Murray was at the door but as he opened it, the sales rep passed by. He cast a quick glance at Murray who nodded and then headed down the staircase. Murray stepped back into the bedroom. "Emily, can you keep an eye on him. I'm not convinced he is a rep. And beside's, I want to try and find his car. You two can help me... please?"

While Emily followed the rep into the dining room, the three of them wandered out into the snow and up the lane.

"Can one of you take a quick look inside that van

parked back there? Just incase we're missing something."

"That one?" Murray had no idea where Ali was pointing but there was only one van. "Oakey dokey."

"While you're searching for these women, how about I go and have a chat with Emily's sister? Save you time Murray."

"Do you think you can find her?" he asked Rita as they slowly climbed the lane.

"Hopefully. If she's still around she must know what happened to her."

"Yeah, good idea, thanks Rita hun. Catch you back here later?"

"OK." And so she was gone.

"Lots of bottles and ciggies Murray mate. No

women! Talking of which, what did you do with her? Only turned my back for a minute!"

"She's gone hunting for Emily's sister. You coming with me or going with her? It's up to you Ali, I'm easy."

"I'll stick with you for a bit. Besides, she wants me to have a man to man chat with you. Think you know what about?"

"Hmm. Don't think I want to know."

"Murray mate, what are you up to? We thought you and Jen were solid?"

"We are... It's just... I can't be me, I can be more honest with Michelle."

"You're not making sense man."

"It's complicated.... Believe me, it's very complicated."

"As long as you know what you're doing Murray my man?"

"No idea! Not a bloody clue!"

Ali left Murray soon after that. Valerie's car was still buried in snow. Murray reached the crossroads and stopped. Which way should he go? If the rep's car was straight on then it was way passed his own Mondeo. He had seen the outline of farm buildings in the distance to the left and the chimney smoke had come from the right. The midnight jeep had also gone to the right. So to the right it was.

There wasn't any sign of the tracks that he had seen earlier but then again, the snow had continued to fall. Emily had said she couldn't remember seeing any footprints near her sister's body. Had they been covered just as quickly? The lane dropped down over a ridge and Murray found his feet slipping on the frozen ground. Maybe Celia had slipped? Slipped and hit her head and then fallen into the stream? An accident? It was a possibility? His mind was turning over but his feet suddenly came to a standstill. Further down the lane was a young pretty Indian woman. Shani. She stopped and glared at him.

 "I'm not going! I'm not going back! You can't make me!" she shouted at him. Murray stood opened-mouthed.

 "I'm not going to make you go anywhere. I haven't got a clue what you're talking about! I don't even know who..." Murray felt a sudden pain shoot through his jaw. The next thing he knew, he was on his side face to face with the snow-covered ground. He shook his head and glanced upwards. There stood beside him was a young angry looking man. Murray hadn't seen him before. With fist still clenched the man spoke through gritted teeth.

"You can tell Sanjiv she's staying with me, right?"

"Who is Sanjiv? Look..." Murray slowly got to his feet, holding his hands out submissively in front of him. "I might be a private investigator, but I'm not working, I'm only here because I took a detour to miss an accident. I really don't know what you are on about." Murray looked the man in the eye. "I don't know who she is and I don't know who you are and I don't know who Sanjiv is, ok?"

The man seemed to relax a little but still stared intensely at Murray.

"Who are you then?"

"My name's Murray Barber. If she want's to stay with you then that's fine with me."

Still the man stared but now he offered a hand to Murray.

"Sorry. I shouldn't have hit you but I panicked. Are you ok?" Murray nodded and glanced over at Shani.

"Is she ok? I saw her jumper in the remains of that fire and thought she might have been hurt?"

"No. She's fine. Do you want to put some ice on that?"

Murray looked at the man, was he being funny? The ground was full of ice.

"I wouldn't mind washing the blood off before I go back to the inn." He could feel the blood trickling down from his lip to his chin.

"Sure, come in. We'll explain. Shani, give us a hand." The two of them led him into the cottage at the bottom of the hill. Sat infront of the roaring woodburner, Shani gently sponged Murray's face.

"It's not too bad. Danny you shouldn't have hit him."

"I'll be alright. Who are you hiding from anyway? Who's this Sanjiv?"

"He's my Uncle. I've only met him once. He's come over from Pakistan with an offer of marriage for me, not to my Uncle but someone he knows. My Father thought it was a good idea, a wealthy man who would give me a good life."

"But I take it that's not what you want?"

"No, we want to stay together." It was the man who spoke.

"So why are you hiding? Surely you can say no?"

"It's not that simple. Family business. Cath, at the inn? Is my best friend's Aunt. We thought we'd be safe hiding down here out of the way for a bit. Then you turned up." Shani lowered her gaze.

"Sorry about that! Where are you from?"

"Bristol. We thought the fire might throw you off the scent."

"That was a bad idea really. Someone could have got hurt. Not us! We left the inn earlier and came down here. This is a holiday cottage that they rent out for most of the year. The weather meant it was empty, which was handy. It's been nice just the two of us here mind." The young man put a protective arm around his girlfriend.

"Well, I have no intention of interfering. I'm just

glad you're safe and well. I thought at first I was seeing things when they all denied knowing anything about you but after the fire I did get concerned."

"That why you came down here looking for us?" The man poured out hot drinks for the three of them.

"No, I was looking for that sales rep's car. There's another woman gone missing and by process of elimination, I think he may have something to do with it."

"Get out! You sure you haven't just got a fertile imagination?" The man was stifling a laugh.

"You know, I'm not sure anymore? I just hope she is alright?" Murray got to his feet. "Look, I'll leave you two alone. But please, believe me, I'm not involved in any family search for either of you, ok?"

CHAPTER SEVEN

Murray arrived back at the inn to be met at the door by Cath.

"Are you alright Mr Barber? Come through to the kitchen, we better explain ourselves." Murray followed her silently, glancing at the sales rep who was still sat at his dinner table in the corner of the dining room. Was Emily still around? Unless she spoke he'd never know. Once in the kitchen, where they found Jim and Karenza loading the dishwasher, Murray turned and started to speak.

"Look, you really don't need to explain yourselves to me..."

"No, I think we should." Jim had a strong west country accent. "You didn't deserve to be thrown into the middle of this. Ahh, we're not used to all this deceiving and what have you."

"Mr Barber, Shani is my niece's best friend.."

"Yeah she said..."

"...Well, as you've probably already gathered, she's hiding down here away from her family. She would have been happy for an arranged marriage if only she hadn't met Danny. Sorry about him hitting you, he phoned just after you left them. He's become quite protective over her but he's just scared he'll lose her I think."

"The fire was a stupid idea. We all panicked last

night." Jim had on glasses and he was peering at Murray over the top of them. "We got this half-brained idea in our heads that it would make you think she had gone and left. Could have got someone hurt."

"Mind you, you were very good at putting that fire out! Ever thought of becoming a fireman?" smiled Karenza.

"No, I can't say I have. But really, stop apologizing, I'm ok. To be honest, I'm just relieved Shani is alright. Unlike the other lady, Valerie Hooper, who knows what's happened to her?"

"She hasn't been back all day has she Mum?"

"No, we haven't seen sight nor sound of the maid. Maybe I should check her room and call the authorities?"

"It might be an idea? The only person here who I think could have had something to do with her disappearance is the rep." All three stood and stared at Murray with bewildered expressions. "Miss Hooper was running from some people. She told me she thought she was being followed, and then she disappeared."

"Oh my!" Cath looked horrified. Whether it was just the situation that Murray had put to her or whether it was the fact it was happening at her inn, Murray wasn't sure?

"Phone the police by all means. And keep an eye on that sales rep!"

"You can er... free drinks in the bar tonight Mr Barber, on the house." It was a welcome comment from Jim as Murray headed back upstairs.

Back in his room once more, Murray collapsed on his bed. His exhaustion was catching up with him. But could he rest while Valerie was still missing?

"Murray are you asleep?" Rita was whispering near his ear. He opened his eyes and sat up slowly.

"Sleep? What's that?" It was a feeble attempt at humour.

"We've brought company."

"Oh right. Celia?" Now Murray was wide awake again.

"No man, we haven't found her yet but this is Giles Barrett. He worked at Dart Farm with the brother, William."

"Giles, hello." Murray instinctively went to pull his notebook out of his pocket but remembered it was sat on his desk at home. He'd just have to remember what was said to him. "Have you got something to tell us?"

"Well sir, I don't know about that? I got only what I know of the Tremwalls. That's who you be asking about isn't it. That maid that was supposed to have done her sister in?"

"Emily yes, but she didn't kill her sister. Did you know the family well?"

"Worked for years with William. He was a good worker, pulled his weight. Just drank too much afterwards! Got into a few rumbles.. huh ha!" Giles let out a short splutter of laughter. "Didn't go down well with old Mr Tremwall. Wanted his son to grow up a bit before he took the reins of the inn. Now James, he was married to Celia, the one that got killed, he thought he could run that place. He used to come over the farm and stir up William. Get him mad so he'd get himself in more trouble. William didn't like him and told him there was no way he was stealing his inheritance! No love lost between those two."

"So it would seem. But would either of them have had any reason to kill Celia?"

"Ah, I don't know about that. William had a temper, but never with his sisters. James was controlling, the jealous sort. But then he had the pretty wife and the family business, why should he risk throwing it all away? Beyond me?"

"Do you remember the day of the murder?"

"It was when we had snow. We were busy on the yard with the livestock."

"Was William with you?"

"Yes, he was there all day. Until dark. We didn't hear about Celia till we arrived at the inn for our evening tipple."

"Well, if he was with you all day, then he didn't kill his sister. Did you see her when she came for groceries?"

"Celia? Yeah sir. She always stopped for a chatter. Very friendly she was. Not aware of her beauty, or the effect she could have on a young man."

"You liked her?"

"Everyone did sir. Can't rightly believe someone would deliberately hurt her."

"Mmm? Maybe nobody did? Maybe she slipped on the snow and fell into the water?"

"Now that would be a good thing? Not that she died but that no-one hurt the maid."

"Mmm." Murray wasn't sure. "Thankyou for coming anyhow. You've been very helpful." Well, he had, it couldn't have been William if he was at the farm all day.

As Murray sat turning his thought's over in his mind, his phone rang. It was Jenny.

"Hi Babe." he answered.

"Hi! I'm off to bed in a minute so I just thought I'd phone and say goodnight. Are you still st...stuck in the snoooow?" Jenny was sounding a little worse for wear.

"You sound like you're having a good time. Yes I am still snowed in. How's the shopping going?"

"Ahhh, great. I've bought you a fantastic kimono..no." giggles rippled down the phone. "Oh, If we get back on Thursday, if we can land.... if the weather's st..still bad, don't come and get me. I'll stay in Exeter. I'll stay at Gareth's flat in town. He said I can stay there. So don't you drive in the snow."

"Well, how about we worry about that on Thursday eh, hun? You sound like you've been enjoying yourself?"

"Oh yes. I'm having a wonderful time! It's spity, it's sapity, it's a pity you are stuck. I miss you you know? It would be nice if you were here too."

"I miss you too babe. I think you could do with getting into bed now by the sound of it. I'm glad you're enjoying yourself even if you are supposed to be working!"

"Ok, I'll go to bed now. I love you hunny." She finished by blowing kisses down the phone.

Murray sat on the edge of his bed and stared at the window. Was that raindrops hitting the pain? He got up and strolled over so to see outside. It was dark but the raindrops were clear enough. At last, it was raining, hopefully the snow would be washed away by morning? Was that someone outside? He could see someone moving at the corner of the building. Probably Finlay checking his van again! No, it wasn't. The body shape was all wrong. It was willowy Mr Sales rep, and he was checking the ground. He wanted to know if the snow was going to melt under the rainfall? It looked like Murray would have to be ready for an early morning start. Before then, however, he was going to make the most of the landlord's generous offer of a free drink or two.

CHAPTER EIGHT

Down in the bar Murray found the couple, Samantha and Colin, having a quiet drink in the corner. The arguing over for now, at least until they managed to get home. Would they fight for their marriages or split and set up a new life together? Murray had absolutely no idea. Finlay was sat at the end of the bar with a pint and reading a newspaper which Murray noticed was from the previous weekend. As Murray sat himself down at the other end of the bar, the sales rep appeared at the front door. Jim poured a glass of house red as Murray studied the rep. Was he a genuine sales rep? He looked smart enough at first glance. Shirt and trousers. But as he shook the rain from his jacket did Murray spot a tattoo on the inside of the man's wrist? Not exactly evidence? If only Murray could find that car?

Murray took a large mouthful of his wine and turned to look at the old photo behind the bar.

"So which one was the murder victim?" he asked Jim who was himself enjoying a pint.

"That one there I do believe. And that one's the sister who killed her."

"I didn't kill her! Why don't you tell him!" Ah, so Emily was still around. Murray couldn't, or at least wouldn't, answer her infront of the landlord and other guests. Instead he continued to study the photo. It was very typical of it's day, early twenties. The men in stiff suits and the women in their Sunday best. Murray was looking more at the faces. Did they give anything away? The parents looked proud. The brother, William, had a look of resentment upon his face. James, Celia's husband had a frown on his face and his hand was placed firmly on his wife's shoulder. She in turn, sat infront of her husband, had an expression that Murray couldn't quite place. Serene? Contented? No, certainly not. A touch of torment there maybe? Maybe he was just seeing what he wanted to see? Maybe it was just the haunted expression of a person who would end their life at the hands of another? Now he was just being melodramatic, she could have slipped as far as he knew.

He finally looked at Emily. She had a genuine looking smile across her face. A touch of cheekiness about it. She looked happy. It was a shame how thing's would turn out...

Murray decided on a second glass before he headed up to bed. It wasn't late but he didn't want to give in to the temptation of too many drinks, he didn't know what time he might have to get up in the morning if Mr sales rep decided to head off early. As he climbed the stairs for the umpteenth time that day, his tired, wine filled mind drifted to thoughts of Jenny. Her shopping trip with Gareth, her social evening out and her soon to be night in his flat. He felt a wave of jealousy rise within him. He opened his bedroom door and sat down heavily on his bed. He should shower and get some sleep.

Maybe just a quick call to Michelle? 'No, go shower' he told himself.

The shower did him good. He realized he couldn't start looking for silly excuses to blame Jenny for his own actions. As he sat back on his bed however, he noticed a message on his phone. It was from Michelle. Without hesitating, he checked to see what she said.

'Dead quiet due to snow. Calling it an early night at work. Are you home yet?'

"Bugger!" he muttered to himself. Should he call her? Why was he even asking? He knew he would...

"Hello." She sounded pleased to hear his voice.

"Hello. I just got your message. I'm still stuck out here in the snow."

"Oh no! Will you ever get home?"

"Hopefully this rain will clear the roads by the morning."

"You sound tired, are you ok?"

"I'm shattered! Sorry, don't mean to sound off or anything. I've been thumped this afternoon, got knocked right off my feet.."

"Oh Murray! Are you alright? You sound like you need some TLC. If you get back tomorrow I'll look after you and make you feel better." Murray didn't answer. "Murray? ... Look, if you're not comfortable with this, I can back off? If you don't want to cheat on Jenny I'll understand. I'd just rather know now than later... I just didn't think you'd even entertain me if everything was so good between you two?... I'm only after some fun, I'm not asking for any sort of commitment so I don't want you to throw away the rest of your life. Please just tell me know before I do get 'involved'..."

Again Murray didn't answer, he was fighting to say what he wanted to say instead of just saying what he knew he should say. "Ok, look, I'll tell you what, if you want to see me tomorrow why don't you ring me when you get home? And if you don't call I won't be offended ok? ... I like you Murray. I know I'm out of order but I can't help it..."

"Michelle.."

"Yeah?"

"... I will call you tomorrow." He said it quietly and then hung up.

He laid on his bed for a good ten minutes trying to decide whether he should call her back? Why hadn't he just said 'I like you, I like being with you, to hell with the right and wrong'? He didn't get the chance though as there was a gentle tap at his door. It was Cath and in her hand was a burgundy coloured handbag. Murray recognized it as the one Valerie had brought with her.

"Mr Barber, can I come in?" she asked. Murray stood back and allowed her to step inside his room. "We're not sure what to do. We've found this handbag in Miss Hooper's room. Jim's gone downstairs to call the police but where is she? If she's out in the snow somewhere she'll die."

"Don't worry, the authorities will know what to do."

"You seem to know more about her than anyone, do you have any idea what could have happened to her? You said something about that sales rep?" her voice had lowered to a whisper.

"I really don't know if he has anything to do with it. You see, Valerie told me she had witnessed a murder, back in Manchester. And the men who did it saw her. So she's on the run, trying to hide from them." Murray was also whispering but he wasn't sure why? "Mr Finlay is smuggling contraband, that's why he keeps checking his van.."

"Oh dear!" Cath sounded shocked.

"Don't worry, I doubt he's dangerous and I've already notified a friend of mine in C.I.D. That couple are just a pair of lovers who are worried about getting caught which just leaves the rep. He could be completely innocent."

"Oh?"

"She went missing last night when Shani sneaked

off with Danny in that jeep. Did you see anyone else out there when they went?"

"No. It was dead quiet out there. Mind you, we did cause a bit of a scene when we set that fire. Do you think she might have been taken during all that fuss? Mr Smith was helping put the fire out, he couldn't have taken her then? That damn fire was such a bad idea."

"Mr Smith? Did he have any I.D.?" Murray raised his eyebrows in disbelief.

"Well, we didn't really check any identities, what with the weather and all. Do you think it's an alias? But then when did he take her?"

"She was only with me in the late evening. He would have had plenty of time during the early hours, either before or after Shani left. Thing is, whoever took her, we don't know where they've taken her or what they've done with her?"

"Oh dear." Cath had gone quite white.

Murray wanted to reassure her that she probably wasn't dead, he was assuming that if she died quite nearby, then Ali and Rita would know something about it, but he couldn't be sure and he wasn't going to try and explain his gift of hearing the dead to his landlady.

"Like I said, there's not a lot we can do right now. You're doing the right thing reporting her missing. Let the authorities do their thing and don't worry." Murray made himself a mental note to ask Ali and Rita to go out and search the local area as soon as they next got back, and hopefully find Valerie's whereabouts...

CHAPTER NINE

After Cath had finally left his room, an exhausted Murray laid back down on his bed. He'd tried to focus his mind on Jenny, letting himself wander down memory lane to when they had first met. Kate had first introduced them at her and Jeff's wedding. Murray had been best man and Jenny at that time had been dating Kate's cousin, Nigel. She had black hair with pink tips, but she had informed him that it was actually midnight blue with fushia tips. They had clicked but that was that until a couple of months later when Kate had asked Murray if she could give his number to Jenny. She had rang, they had arranged to meet up and thing's just sort of swam along happily. She was fun and sometimes a little unpredictable! He had never told her about his gift, and neither had Jeff or Kate even though they both knew. Yet they had managed to get along fine in they're seemingly separate lives. Had their relationship progressed in the last three years? Not a lot. It had stayed pretty much on the same level. That raised the question why? Why had he not taken it to the next level? He already knew the answer. How could he commit to someone who knew so little about him? Who knew nothing of his everyday existence? It wasn't her fault, he had never shared it with her. She knew nothing of Ali or Rita. Did he not trust her enough to share it with her? He always seemed to use the excuse that she would either laugh at him or scream at him for keeping secrets. They were feeble excuses. Michelle was right, everything was not perfect between them. Yet, as he let his mind continue along it's path, with Michelle things were easy. Easier? Things such as honesty and believing him when he spoke of such fantastic possibilities as the likes of ghosts. He didn't even have to think about it with Michelle, it was just natural. So what should he do?

"Murray my man! You awake there?" Ali's voice rang through Murray's head bringing him abruptly back to the present. "You got company!"

Murray sat up and stared around his empty room.

"Hello? Who's here Ali?"

"Murray mate, say hello to Celia Gidleigh."

"Celia? You found her, well done! Hello Celia." Murray turned and sat on the side of his bed facing the window, which was still being splattered with raindrops and was where the voices were coming from.

"Hello. You're Mr Barber? You've been speaking to my sister Emily? Is she here?" Celia's voice was soft and sweet.

"She's around here somewhere. Rita? Are you here? Do you want to go and find her? Drag her back if you have too!"

"Ok. I'll go and find her." Rita set off in search of Emily.

"So, Celia, what happened to you? We know it wasn't Emily. It'd be nice to hear you slipped in the snow, not nice for you but .. well you know what I mean?"

"Yes, I think I do. But I'm afraid I can't say that." Celia's voice came close beside Murray, she had sat herself down on the bed next to him.

"It wasn't your sister and it couldn't have been your brother as he was at the farmyard all day with Giles. So, that doesn't leave a lot of options, not unless some stranger came along and knocked you into the water for fun."

"No, that didn't happen either."

"Come on maid, out with it. Tell us who you met down in the ravine." Ali was still near the window.

"It was a freezing cold day, I had been to the farm and seen Giles and Billy. I always stayed too long but we used to lose track of the time chatting. Giles used to make me laugh a lot. It was foolish of me, I should have known better really, James always got so mad when he didn't know where I was..."

"James? Your husband? But he did know where you were, you'd gone to get supplies..."

"He always questioned me. Everytime I went anywhere. He was convinced I was being courted by other men."

"I thought he was out getting a half pig that day?" Murray was trying to recall what he had already been told, not so easy without his trusted notebook.

"He was. He had already collected it. Then he had decided to collect me from the farm, save me walking in the snow. Except he saw me before he got there, from the top of the lane. And then he got it into his mind that I should already have been home by then, so why had it taken me so long? I told him I'd got chatting to the men and that just got him riled. He pushed me and I slipped... I did slip, but then he just got madder because I'd dropped the eggs and then he hit me and I fell against the rocks and then I remember seeing him reach out to me... but he wasn't helping me up, he was grabbing my neck and then I felt myself getting colder, so cold and the freezing water running down my throat ... and I started to choke..."

"It's ok. You don't have to go any further." Murray spoke quietly.

"Celia." It was Emily's voice coming from behind them, near the door. "Oh Celia! Forgive me, I would never have hurt you."

Murray smiled to himself. The two sister's were finally reunited after nearly a century. If it turned out to be the only good thing that came of these few days, it would be enough. All he wanted now was to get some sleep....

CHAPTER TEN

Sleep was not something that was coming easy to Murray. Maybe he just needed his own bed? Or maybe it was the whereabouts of Valerie Hooper that was playing on his mind? Either way, he managed about three hours total before he was awoken by a voice urgently screaming into his ear.

"Murray! Murray mate, wake up!"

"Ali?" Murray stirred slowly.

"Wake up Murray! Old sales rep guy is on the move. We followed him to his car..."

"Where was it?" Murray was wide awake all of a sudden. "What about Valerie?"

"Get moving man and I'll tell you..." Murray got out of bed and started pulling on his trousers and top. "He had the car, a nice BMW, hidden just behind some stone walling along the lane by the farm. You couldn't see it from the road even if you had gone along that way...."

"What about Valerie? Is she with him? Is she alright?"

"He started his car and drove it back along the lane, we hitched a lift, see where he was going. Then we heard some clumping in the boot, like something heavy moving, so we stuck our heads in there, thought it might be some samples of whatever he's supposed to be selling, but it wasn't, it was Miss Hooper! Unconscious and covered in a blanket..."

"Unconscious? Not dead?"

"No man, she's still on your side, just. Anyway, he stopped the car at the top of the track down to the ravine. That's when I split to come and get you. Come on, while he's still nearby." Murray was already on his way downstairs with his phone in his jacket pocket. Should he stop and wake Jim and Cath? There may not be time? He was out the front door and running up the pitch black lane, the snow like slush under his shoes.

"Which is the quickest way to the ravine? I take it he's stopped there to get rid of her?"

"Follow my voice, we can cut across the field here, don't slip..."

As they reached the other side of the field, they could hear the sound of a car engine start up and pull away. Still following the sound of Ali's voice, Murray slid his way down the last of the track to the sound of running water.

"Murray! Ali! Hurry, she's down here!" Rita called out from the blackness. Murray followed her cries, his heart pounding inside his chest. "She's here, her face is in the water! He knocked her head on the rocks aswell Murray, quick!" Murray stumbled into the water. The freezing cold feeling like a stabbing knife attacking his ankles. He pulled her head from the water and dragged her to the edge. He grabbed his phone from his pocket and dialled 999.

"Ambulance." He yelled at the operator. "Air ambulance if it's possible. I've got a woman here with a head wound and unconscious, she's been out in this weather for about twenty-four hours!....."

Having given all the required information, Murray pulled off his jacket and wrapped it around the cold body of Miss Hooper. He could feel a pulse but it wasn't a strong one. With all his strength, he picked her up in both arms and started the trek back up the track to the top of the hill, guided only by the sound of Ali and Rita's voices. He could only hope that the ambulance would be able to make it along the roads, and that it wouldn't take too long.....

It had been four-thirty when he had trooped out into the night to help Valerie Hooper, it was now six in the morning and Murray was wrapped up in a fleece blanket in front of a roaring open fire in the private lounge at the inn. His wet clothes were being washed and dried by Cath who had also provided a hot coffee with a dash of brandy.

"I can't believe how lucky she was, you following that Mr Smith like that. You must have sat up all night waiting for him to make his move Mr Barber. Thank God the ambulance was able to get through ok. Let's just hope there's no complications now that they've got her to the hospital. Did she say anything to you Mr Barber? What he'd done to her?"

"No." Murray barely had a voice. "She was totally out for the count. He must have taken her during the night, night before last, and kept her knocked out somehow in the boot of his car. Although I doubt anybody would have heard her even if she had been conscious."

"Oh she must have been terrified. You know, I didn't like the look of him the minute I set eyes on him. Sales rep my foot!" She turned back towards Murray after placing another log on the fire. "Do you think they'll get him?"

"I called my friend in C.I.D., the one I mentioned to you before, I gave him the license plate number. Hopefully that'll help." Murray wasn't going to add that it had been his dead friends who had given him the information. "Apparently his real name is Smith, Aaron Smith and he's well known up Manchester way. Got a list of offences to his name including ABH, robbery, attempted murder..."

"Could be up for that one again then with any luck."

"He needs to be put away for good by the sound of it." Murray agreed.

"Make's you wonder why he took her down the ravine? He must have overheard us talking about the photo in the bar, thought it would be poetic for history to repeat itself I suppose?" Cath had sat back on her knees and heels but after a moment's thought she struggled back up onto her feet. "I know one thing, after this week, I'm going to be very careful how I judge my guests and what I say infront of them!"

"I agree, this has been a few days out of my life I could do without repeating. If my girlfriend ever asks again for a lift to the airport, I'm gonna book her a taxi!"

With warm, dry, clean clothes and a hot full English breakfast inside of him, Murray settled his bill, and made a payment to cover Valerie's, and then graciously accepted a lift from Jim back up to his car. The rain wasn't heavy but he didn't particularly want to get wet all over again.

The snow hadn't cleared completely and what was still left covering the ground was a dirty grey but it was slushy underfoot and that meant drivable upon. Jim waited for Murray to start his engine and pull away safely and then with a final toot, the two men set off in their separate directions.

Murray's mind fixed itself on what he was going to do when he reached home. He had been swaying back and forth between Jenny and Michelle. He felt a loyalty to Jenny but he also knew he had already torn a massive hole into that. If he was totally honest with himself he knew their future would consist of the sort of relationship that they were already experiencing. Not that that was such a bad thing. He had been completely content until Michelle had shown up on the scene. But, again with complete honesty, that told him what he had wasn't necessarily what he really wanted. As Michelle had said, if all was perfect in paradise.... but then again, was there such a thing as the perfect relationship? After all, Michelle was fun and exciting now... but three years down the line, where would they be? The one decision Murray came to was that he wasn't good at making decisions!

'Bugger, what the hell' he thought. I'll phone Michelle when I get in and just see how thing's go, I've already cracked the egg anyhow...

Murray didn't see the black ice as his car suddenly spun across the road leaving him no more than a passenger as he felt himself thrown against the inside of his car door. The sky became a grey white colour as the lose items that lay beside him flew into the air. Time around him seemed to slow as a trail of thoughts shot through his mind... Was this it? Death on the bleak, lonely moor, having just saved somebody else's life? Is that what they mean when they say we're all here for a reason and when your time comes around, that's it? Ali's take on his own crash had been 'puncture, ditch, tree'. Would Murray's be 'ice, snow, hard place'? The final thought he had before the blackness took over him, was 'will it be Ali and Rita who meet him on the otherside........?

L - #0180 - 130519 - C0 - 210/148/7 - PB - DID2515509